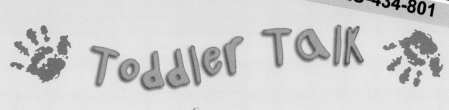

Toddler Talk

Yuk!

Written by Nicola Baxter
Illustrated by Jan Lewis

ARMADILLO

This is Humphrey.

He likes painting

and he adores splashing

and he loves snoozing.

But when it comes to food, he has only
one thing to say…

Yuk!

"Just a little teensy, weensy bit, darling," urges his mother.

Yuk!

"Here comes the big aeroplane. Vrooooom!" says his father.

Yuk!

"Hurry up, Humph. It's not that bad," says his big sister.

But Humphrey puts his snout in the air.

Yuk! Yuk! Yuk! Yuk! Yuk! Yuk! Yuk! Yuk!

So his mother makes

a funny face

a funny fish

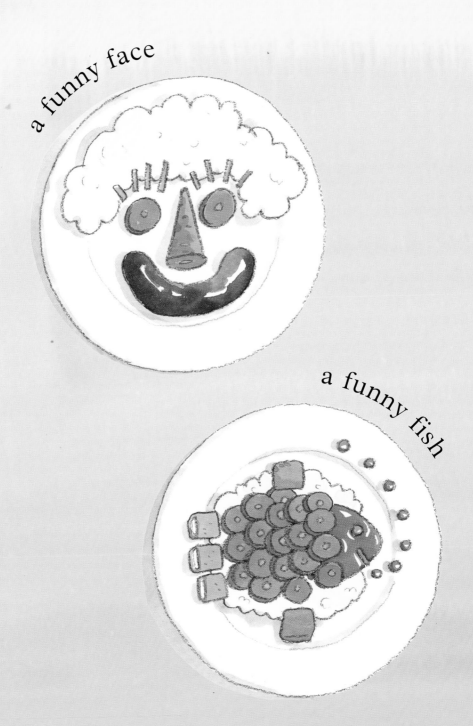

and some funny fingers!

Humphrey doesn't think they are funny.

Yuk!

Humphrey's father tries to take a firm trotter with his son.

"You must eat this to grow up big and strong like me," he says. "Now be a good piglet."

Humphrey only has one thing to say about that.

Humphrey doesn't like his breakfast.

He doesn't like his lunch.

He doesn't like his supper.

His parents despair.

Then, one day, someone is suddenly very, very...

hungry.

"What a relief!" sigh his mother and father and big sister. But Humphrey doesn't say anything...